ENVY

ALAIN ELKANN

ENVY

Translated from the Italian
by Alastair McEwen

PUSHKIN PRESS
LONDON

English translation © Alastair McEwen 2007

First published in Italian as
L'invidia © Romanzo Bompiani 2006

This edition first published in 2007 by
Pushkin Press
12 Chester Terrace
London N1 4ND

British Library Cataloguing in Publication Data:
A catalogue record for this book is available
from the British Library

ISBN (13) 978 1 901285 81 9
ISBN (10) 1 901285 81 2

Cover: *La Poupée* Hans Bellmer 1936
© DACS/Bridgeman Art Library

Frontispiece: Alain Elkann
© Jean-Philippe Baltes/SIPA PRESS

Set in 12 on 18 Baskerville Monotype
and printed in Jordan
by National Press

To Leone

PART ONE

CHANCE ENCOUNTERS

1

LONDON

THE FIRST TIME I SAW JULIAN SAX he was having dinner with Damian Oxfordshire in a restaurant on Brompton Road and I noticed how the two men seemed satisfied to be in each other's company. I don't know why that blurred image has remained impressed on my memory.

2

MADRID

A T THE ITALIAN CULTURAL INSTITUTE, a run-
down building only a short distance from the
Cathedral, one evening I ate with Matteo Esse and
Charles Bloom, who was in Madrid to make a docu-
mentary on Velázquez. Matteo Esse is an influential
man in the world of Italian culture. An intransi-
gent, excitable controversialist, he was suggesting
with great insistence that Bloom take on the artistic
direction of the Venice Biennale. Bloom was non-
committal, but it was clear that he was gratified by
the idea and he let Matteo Esse flatter him as he
drank glass after glass of Spanish red. At a certain
point, I don't exactly remember why, the conversation moved on to Julian Sax. They talked about
him enthusiastically; both of them thought he was

the greatest living artist and felt that it would be only right to organise an exhibition of Sax's work in Venice as soon as possible. It could be presented as an exceptional event within the context of the Biennale. I must say that I was curious and even amazed at how seriously Bloom took Esse's proposal to direct the Biennale. Perhaps he had already thought of this position on other occasions. He became so absorbed by this prospect that he even reeled off a list of practical problems that might have hampered the project. Matteo Esse listened to these arguments with indifference; Bloom's practical requirements didn't strike him as important because he knew that solutions could be found. The main thing was that Bloom be selected to direct the Biennale. It would have been a fantastic coup because his was a most authoritative and intelligent voice in the field of contemporary art, a solitary voice and one averse to passing fashions. The two men got along well and thought highly of each other precisely because they detested the fashionable and the commonplace. Both were hot-blooded and subject to unpredictable mood swings.

3

NEW YORK

A FEW MONTHS LATER, we went with Matteo
Esse to visit Bloom in his Soho apartment.
It was a large loft furnished only with bookshelves
and piles of books scattered about, two sofas uphol-
stered in white canvas and a table with two chairs.
Charles, dressed in white, was in high spirits and
said openly that he was ready to come to Italy. But
things had gone otherwise and at the Biennale they
had appointed another director whose idea of contemporary art was poles apart from that of Charles
Bloom and Matteo Esse. So, despite repeated telephone calls and messages, for a long time Charles
Bloom took no further part in our lives and became
inaccessible. Perhaps he had taken umbrage or perhaps he had forgotten about it, throwing himself

into another project. Matteo Esse continued to deplore the failure to choose Bloom as a terrible shame and lack of vision.

4

ROME

I HAD A VISIT FROM PAUL, an English friend and a well known journalist who had to write a piece on Italian politics and wanted some advice on how to go about things and whom to meet. I asked him:

"How are you? How's life?"

"Great, I have a young wife and a little boy. At my age it's all terribly exciting."

"When did you get married?"

"Two years ago, with Lidia Sax. Maybe you met her when she lived in Italy."

"Yes, she's Julian's daughter. Do you know her father well?"

"Yes."

"I've been hearing a lot about him recently and I felt like interviewing him."

"I don't think that'll be too easy, he hates giving interviews."

"Could you help me out?"

"Yes, of course, I'll tell Lidia as soon as I get back to London."

5

LONDON

I CALLED PAUL, but he had given me a wrong number. The people who answered were strange, ill at ease, as if they knew and didn't want to say anything. I felt I had been deliberately misled, until a mutual friend gave me the right number. I spoke with Paul and Lidia, who suggested I write a letter to her father. She would take it to him, but she told me straight off that she could guarantee me nothing. Then she asked me kindly:

"Would you like to have lunch with Paul and me tomorrow?"

I accepted because I felt like spending time with them and because I wanted to get a better idea of who Julian Sax really was. But then Lidia called me again late that evening:

"I'm sorry, but it won't be possible to meet up because I have to go to Brighton with my son. We'll do it another time. I'll let you know if my father replies, but as I told you I wouldn't get your hopes up. He avoids interviews and in any case he never has the time."

One evening, in the home of some English friends, I met a gentleman who was a splendidly ironic, inexhaustible conversationalist. On learning that I was Italian and worked in the art field, he asked:

"Do you know Matteo Esse, by any chance?"

"Yes, we're friends."

"I haven't seen him in ages. We met in Venice years ago; he was very young, extraordinary. He took us to see splendid things that aren't very well known and he had a fascinating way of talking about art. What happened to him?"

"He's fine, still the same, always engaged in thousands of battles! He wanted Charles Bloom to direct the Biennale and organise an exhibition of Julian Sax's work, but it didn't come off."

"Of course, Sax is a very special artist and an exhibition in Venice would have been marvellous, but with that character of his goodness knows if he would have agreed."

"Do you know him?"

"Yes, very well."

"I'd like to meet him, interview him. I tried through his daughter Lidia, but it doesn't seem easy."

"I don't know how much influence Lidia has. I think you should look him up, take him a bottle of fine French red wine. Very expensive wine."

"But I don't even know his address!"

"Go to Tony's, it's a tea shop near Notting Hill Gate. He's there every morning at nine."

"What's he like?"

"You can't say he's an easy man. He has an ambiguous relationship with money and with women. He is very reserved and arrogant too, in a certain sense. But he is undoubtedly an extraordinary artist. He is very capricious and moody, but remember, if you wish to speak with him, the best thing is to take him a bottle of the finest French wine. You'll see, it's the only way."

"But if I don't know him, it'll strike him as odd when I show up with a bottle of wine in a café first thing in the morning!"

"Don't try to be logical, follow my advice. You've nothing to lose, and you'll see that I'm right."

I called Damian Oxfordshire, whom I've known for years, because I knew that in the past he had shown Sax's work in his gallery and that they were close friends. I wanted to know if he thought it might be possible to interview Sax. He gave me an evasive reply, saying that he would speak to him but that it wasn't the best time to do so. Then he asked me to drop in at his gallery and I went with Rossa, who had arrived in London in the meantime. Damian has long, white, rather tousled hair and he was wearing a dark blue cashmere jacket with leather buttons, light grey flannels, and a bright blue shirt that highlighted the colour of his eyes. He greeted us in his affected, ironic way, then, as if shaking off his natural indifference, he enthusiastically showed us a Van Gogh from his Saint-Rémy period, sitting on an easel.

"I've just sold it to an American museum. It's very fine, don't you think?"

"Yes, it's wonderful! And that portrait of a woman on the other easel?" I asked him curiously.

"It's a painting by Julian Sax. Oh, I know that you want to interview him, but I'm not sure if that will be possible. He is very tired and I haven't seen him for a bit. The next time you come to London we'll organise a meeting."

"Who is the woman in the portrait?"

"A model who used to live with him and gave him a lot of problems. Julian left her and fell for a fat, imposing black woman, whose portrait he is doing. I know that they have an excessively active sexual relationship, unwise for a man of his age. It's odd, because he's a hypochondriac. But to justify himself to me he says that theirs is first and foremost an intellectual relationship."

"I'd like to interview him because I don't think he is sufficiently well known in Italy."

Damian's attention had wandered from the conversation, he wasn't interested in knowing whether Sax was well known or not in Italy. For him it was merely a boring detail. He said goodbye politely but impatiently, as if he had suddenly felt an urgent need to be on his own:

"So, let me know when you're coming back to London and we can meet up with Julian."

6

ROME

B Y THEN I COULDN'T get the idea of meeting or interviewing Sax out of my mind. I called Damian again to tell him I was coming back to London and to remind him that he had said he would arrange a meeting with Sax.

"I'm sorry but he has had a bad bout of pneumonia and is struggling to get back on his feet. Right now, he's not seeing anyone."

"What's happening with his love affair with the fat woman, the black one?"

"The portrait is finished and so is the affair. The way it always is with him."

"What's the portrait like?"

"Julian is pleased with it: I haven't seen it yet. When are you coming?"

"Next Thursday."

"Unfortunately I shall be in Jamaica."

Perhaps it was true, perhaps it was an excuse, but I understood that there was no longer any point in discussing Sax with Damian.

7

LONDON

E ARLY IN THE MORNING I WENT to Tony's, the café where Matteo Esse's English friend told me I would see Sax. You enter through a baker's and then go down a flight of stairs that leads to a large room with round tables and light-coloured rattan chairs. There were few people about, I ordered a coffee, read the paper and then I asked a waitress who had a kindly look:

"Have you seen Mr Sax?"

"Yes, he was here, but he's already gone."

As I left I noticed that next door there was a shop where they sell pretty much everything. I took a look around and to make things look natural I bought a packet of cigarettes. I asked the Indian man who was sitting behind the counter:

"Do you know Julian Sax by any chance?"

"Yes, he always comes here to buy the papers. He's only just left."

"Where does he live?"

"Around the corner."

I set off along the pavement and spotted a crowd coming and going in front of an antique dealer's where they sold mirrors. I asked:

"Do you know where Mr Sax lives?"

"See those green plants, those clumps of bamboo that hide that dark house?"

"Yes."

"Right, that's where he lives."

I felt intimidated at having attained my goal. Two windows were lit up, one on the ground floor, the other on the first floor. I screwed up my courage, rang the doorbell and shortly after that it was opened by a young man wearing jeans, trainers and a plaid shirt. He had blue eyes and spoke English with an American accent. Looking at me in surprise he asked:

"What do you want?"

"I'd like to talk to Mr Sax."

"I'm sorry, but who are you and who told you that Mr Sax lives here?"

"The man who works in the antique shop where they sell mirrors, here, on this very street."

"Mr Sax has no time, he never receives anyone. Speak to his lawyer."

"I'd like to talk to him, organise an exhibition in Italy for him."

"That's not possible right now."

"I'd like him to hold an exhibition in Venice, he would be supported by two critics who have an unbounded admiration for him, Matteo Esse and Charles Bloom."

"Just a moment, please."

The door was left ajar and I understood that the young man had gone into the room on the ground floor where Sax was. I thought of following him, but I didn't. The boy with the plaid shirt reappeared. He handed me an envelope from the Larry Gagosian Art Gallery on which he had written the name and telephone number of a lawyer to whom I might speak if I needed any information. He said goodbye with a slightly embarrassed smile and closed the black door in my face.

I don't know if Sax had seen me from the window or not. I was disappointed at having got so close to him and having lacked the courage to assert myself.

PART TWO

THE BIRTH OF AN OBSESSION

1

LONDON

As SOON AS I GOT BACK to the hotel, I told Rossa right away about all that had happened and then I called the lawyer, who asked me in brusque and suspicious tones to send her a letter with a clear explanation of my proposal.

Later on we went for a stroll in Hyde Park and at a certain point Rossa asked me to take her to see Sax's house. We passed in front of it in a taxi, then I pointed out Tony's to her. Without a second's hesitation Rossa told the taxi driver to stop:

"Let's go and have lunch there, I bet you we'll meet him."

Sax was sitting at a corner table, drinking tea and eating dry biscuits as he chatted with a young, pregnant woman. Feeling euphoric, we sat down at a table almost in front of them. Rossa looked at him and he looked back. Sax had piercing blue eyes and unkempt, short grey hair. He was wearing an ivory-coloured pullover of an unusual shape, too short and too wide, and around his neck he had knotted a small foulard. I didn't have the courage to get up and go to speak to him. I was intimidated by his presence and wondered, after what had happened a few hours before at his own front door, if he had recognised me. In the meantime he and the young pregnant woman had stood up and were saying goodbye, exchanging a friendly kiss. She wasn't a lover, perhaps she was one of his daughters.

Rossa was shaken, she told me that Sax was a seductive man with a disturbing gaze.

My daughter Sole, who lives in London, had met him some years before during a weekend in the country and had found him disagreeable, garrulous and petulant. She remembered him as a short man, elegant, a heavy smoker. When Rossa and I told her about our encounter, she gave an ironic smile.

I asked her to meet us at eight the next morning for coffee at Tony's. If Sax were to show up, maybe she could introduce me.

I waited for Sole for ten minutes or so, then she came in wearing a dark jacket and a black woollen beret.

She is twenty-five, very pretty, with dark, very expressive eyes. You can tell her state of mind immediately from the look in her eyes.

We went down to the tearoom and ordered coffee. As we waited for Sax we talked about ourselves. She began by saying:

"I know I'm difficult. I like only handsome, weak men. Older men are attracted to me, while I am attracted to younger men. But it's more difficult with younger men. I intimidate them, or maybe I'm too shy and spoil things before they happen."

It was the first time my daughter had spoken to me this way. I no longer felt like a father, we were a man and a woman and I was listening to her talk.

Every so often we would glance absently at the stairs, but Sax didn't appear. Sole said:

"I don't understand why you're so interested in him."

"Maybe because I'm always on the move and he's always in the same place. Maybe because I fritter away my time and he's focussed. Maybe because everything he does is over the top and I'm too cautious. What's more, I'm fascinated by the fact that he is the grandson of Ludwig Sax, the most important scientist of the last century! Maybe I envy him because I would have liked to have his destiny."

"When you were my age, what did you think about love?"

"I always wanted to be bought by a woman. To give her the illusion that she could buy me only to prove to her that it wasn't true, that she had got it wrong. I wanted to pretend I could be bought, but in reality I was free and no one could possess me."

"That seems complicated to me, but I understand you. I too get just so far and then withdraw, I can't help it. It's as if I were protecting myself, as if I had the premonition that in any case I would end up disappointed. You know, I tend to run away from people who might make me suffer."

"I don't think Sax is going to show. Will you come with me to buy some notebooks?"

"Yes, of course, I know a stationer near here where they sell notebooks that are just right for you. Black, slim, with squares, you'll see! Look, do you want to meet him because you want to buy one of his pictures?"

"No, I'd like to interview him, maybe become his friend."

"Are you sure that this obsession of yours doesn't hide a desire to write a book about him?"

"No, as long as he's alive that's impossible."

"Why?"

"Because I would have to tell the whole truth."

"But people write novels because they are imaginary stories, you can tell the truth in them."

"Do you think you'll marry?"

"And do you still want to be possessed? Did my mother possess you?"

"She loved me, then she tired of me and I allowed other women to possess me. Would you like an Italian husband?"

"I'm not sure I want a husband."

"As time passed I gradually wanted different things. Women have taught me all there is to know about life, above all to become myself."

"Where do I stand in your life?"

"You are my daughter, and a unique woman. As my mother was."

"Have I disappointed you?"

"No, but sometimes I get scared because you're so much like me. I'd like you to have a happy life and I wish you were less troubled."

"Are you happy?"

"If I were truly happy I wouldn't be obsessed by Julian Sax. But I've had my moments of happiness."

"I wouldn't like to have a father like Sax, you know I never liked him. I understand that he's fascinating because he's Ludwig Sax's grandson, maybe he's even a real artist, but I'm not too sure about him. He has a certain something that irritates me—I get the feeling he's two-faced."

"But he's a great artist and he's sure of that. Unfortunately, I don't have that certainty. I really envy him. He is a wolf; I don't have the courage to be like that. Why do you think young men don't find you attractive?"

"Because they don't want girls with too many problems, too many questions, too many moods. They want to have fun and feel important."

"Maybe you should look for more mature men, older than you."

"I told you before, I don't like them. I am attracted to handsome, young, weak men."

Going with my daughter to buy notepads was a happy moment for me and I was touched as I watched her making her choice with an expert eye. I felt we had similar tastes.

When we parted I thought I wasn't used to speaking to her that way. I wasn't worried about her being attracted to handsome young men, but because she was too intelligent and was bound to get hurt. Although I had messed up many matters of the heart in my life, I still felt that our relationship was secure.

Rossa, Sole and I went to have breakfast at Tony's on Saturday. Julian Sax was there, sitting at a round table with one of his daughters, a grandson, and his son-in-law. He was a grandfather and an affectionate father, and he seemed very much at ease in those circumstances. We observed the scene, but didn't know how to behave. Sole should have stood up, gone over to him and said:

"Do you remember me?"

Perhaps we should have broken the ice, but all of us were looking awkwardly towards Sax's table.

At a certain point Julian rose to his feet, irritated. He felt he was being watched and he left, giving his daughter a hasty kiss; the others left shortly after. Our silence and our inquisitive stares had disturbed their family get-together.

2

TONY'S

WHY HAD WE SAT THERE HYPNOTISED, without making a move? Why, on finding myself so close to Sax for the second time, had I not gone up to him and asked him if he would grant me an interview? Had I been afraid that he might humiliate me with a refusal? But wasn't it more humiliating, in front of Rossa and Sole, to have lacked the courage to go and speak to him? That man intimidated me, made me feel insecure, paralysed me. I know that this didn't matter to Sole, but I had realised that Rossa was under Sax's spell and, if he had been younger, she might have fallen in love with him. But what did age matter? Sax had erotic episodes, love affairs, with very young women. He would take them to his studio where he seduced them, painted them, and left them. Why did he do this? Why did he need to seduce women so much? The truth was that I didn't make contact with him because I was afraid that even Rossa might have fallen into the net cast by that werewolf. What if he had suggested that he paint her portrait? Perhaps even Sole, who always spoke of him in disparaging terms, might have accepted. I couldn't bear the idea of my wife or daughter sitting for him. Better to get rid of this obsession and put it out of mind. Forget Sax.

PART THREE

WOMEN

1

NEW YORK

I CHANGED MY MIND on reading the *New York Times*, where I found a review of an exhibition of Sax's work at the Sidney Wallace Gallery. Not many paintings: the portrait of the black woman, an officer of the Queen's Grenadier Guards sprawling in a chair, the artist's white dog, a naked male friend lying on a bed, his pregnant daughter, a little grandchild … I was curious to find out if the daughter and the grandson were the ones we had seen in London at Tony's or if it was Lidia with my friend Paul's son.

We went to visit Sidney Wallace. He received us in his office: a big room with three desks and two sofas. We talked about Sax right away. I told him how I had followed Sax various times to suggest that he hold an exhibition in Venice or give me an interview.

I didn't say that we had seen him twice at Tony's and I hadn't dared speak to him. Wallace wouldn't have understood my insecurity. Nor was there any need to speak up in Rossa's presence, because she may have confused my hesitance with my tendency to voyeurism. Without hesitation, Wallace said:

"Not to worry, if Julian is stand-offish and doesn't want to talk there's nothing personal about it. He has no time for interviews. He lives like a monk, and thinks only of painting. He works early in the morning, then takes a break for lunch, has a nap and goes back to work until the small hours. He doesn't want to see anyone, he never gives interviews, and he doesn't even attend the openings of his exhibitions. You have to take him as he comes. He is obsessive and unpredictable. For example, he hates money yet he earns piles of it."

"How much is one of his paintings worth today?"

"It depends, but I'd say several million dollars. But I repeat, he wastes money. For years he played the casinos and the horses just for the fun of losing. You know, not so long ago, in Paris, he took a fancy to a man whose face intrigued him. He started to paint his portrait but then, out of the blue, he changed his mind. He called me in the middle of the night and said: 'I don't like that man anymore, he means nothing to me, I never want to see him again.' 'But he has already paid.' 'Give him his money back.'

"I remember a Swiss banker who wanted Julian to paint his portrait at all costs. Every week he would travel from Zurich to London and sometimes he would pose for hours. Julian made him wait and then maybe he would tell him to come back another time because he didn't feel like working that day. But the banker was so determined to have that portrait that he put up with everything … In the end Julian finished it."

"That seems very arrogant to me," said Rossa in irritation.

Yet I knew that she too would have agreed to sit for him, out of defiance, vanity. She would have made Julian fall in love with her and she would have had the courage to say:

"Please keep the money I have given you, but I don't like the portrait, it doesn't interest me, and I don't want it."

Sidney Wallace talked about Sax as if he were a genius.

"I had wanted to work with him for years. The relationship was forged bit by bit and now I can say that he trusts me."

In saying 'he trusts me' he revealed the pride of a man who had won the great privilege of deciding what should be done with the work of this extraordinary artist. His was the responsibility.

I added:

"I wanted to suggest to him that he hold an exhibition in Venice."

"That's a good idea, but I think someone has already thought of that."

"Who?"

"I don't recall. I would have to ask one of my sons who dealt with that proposal."

"So, if I have understood correctly, someone is already working on an exhibition in Venice and you think it won't be possible to interview Sax?"

"I don't think so, but with him you never know."

I took Rossa to Vladimir's place. He was an American friend of Russian origin whom I hadn't seen for years and whose parents I had met. His mother, Tatiana, was an eccentric who had been playing canasta for a lifetime with another Russian woman, Sonia. They couldn't do without each other, but they also loathed each other because they both claimed to have been Mayakovsky's mistress. That evening in Vladimir's house there were some art critics I hadn't seen for a long time. One of them was an Englishman who lives in New York and has been working on a monumental book on Picasso for years. When I went up to greet him he was talking about Sax to a young man. Not without vanity, he was saying:

"Julian calls me every evening, he wants to know the jet-set gossip here in New York. Either he calls me or he calls Charles Bloom."

I said hello and broke into the conversation, saying straight off:

"I saw Sidney Wallace today, he says that all Sax thinks of is work."

"Yes, he's been like that since he stopped gambling."

2

LONDON

I TOLD SOLE I HAD SEEN Sax's latest pictures in New York and that they had struck me as interesting. She said:

"I got an invitation to spend the weekend at Damian Oxfordshire's place in the country, and I knew Sax was going to be there too."

"But he never leaves London."

"You know he has a soft spot for Damian. But I didn't go because I didn't feel like seeing him."

"Why do you look down on him so much? He's a great artist!"

"That's what you think."

"It's not just me, the market thinks so too."

"I prefer other artists. I prefer Hopper."

"But Hopper is dead."

"So what, Leonardo, Poussin, and Caravaggio are dead too!"

"Okay, let's not argue about it."

Sole is like that. She is not an easy person to understand and she is moody. It's very hard to be accepted by her. Since childhood she has always tried to suppress suffering and worries. She loves her family, but lives far from us because we have too strong an effect on her emotions. She is a woman who needs to be helped to live, but with respect. You have to leave her breathing room, encouraging her and listening to her when she wants it. Besides, with grown up children you must learn to keep a certain distance, and not suffer when they don't see things the way you do. It's not easy, but if I am obsessed by Sax and Sole can't stand him, it's better not to press the point, simply change the subject.

3

PROVENCE

ONE EVENING, Sole and a cousin of hers took us to the home of some English friends, an architect and an antiques dealer. The garden is very well tended, the swimming pool is a small oval affair, and the furnishings spartan. When we were at dinner and the atmosphere was relaxed, a young man who gave off a strong scent of rather spicy cologne started talking about sex, gambling, and homosexual friendships. At a certain point, a distinguished American lady alluded to Julian Sax and the conversation immediately switched to him. His turbulent past, moments of great debauchery, his vast brood of illegitimate children, his rebellious side, and his arrogance, were all subjects that triggered endless anecdotes. The English are puritanical, but they are mad about scandals and gossip. Sax's model was Lord Byron. A great lover of horses, gambling, food, and women.

Sole's cousin, at table with us, said:

"Every time she can, my mother lunches at Tony's because she knows that Julian is there."

"Does she know him?" asked the American lady.

"No, I don't think she has ever spoken to him. My father is afraid of Sax. As a young man he frequented violent company, street thugs."

José, a fellow who had said nothing until then, said:

"Julian is obsessed by museums, especially the museums of Madrid. Bacon had a passion for Madrid too. Besides, the pair of them were close companions for years, until Bacon broke with Sax and began running him down."

Rossa said: "My husband is obsessed by Sax."

José replied:

"He's right, he's a very special man. My friend lived for years near to Sax's place. He knew his model."

"Who? The black lawyer whose portrait he

painted?" I asked curiously, aware that Sole would give me one of her ironic looks.

"No, another woman. Sax's latest pictures are on show at the Wallace Collection and the curator of the exhibition had lunch with him. A few hours later, he wrote her a letter asking if he could paint her portrait. At first, she thought it was a joke. When she understood that it was true, she had no time to sit for him. She takes her work really seriously and he expects his models to give him unlimited time."

Rossa said: "She certainly missed a unique opportunity."

"Would you like Sax to do your portrait?" asked José.

"Who wouldn't?"

"What kind of man is Sax?" asked one of our hosts.

"An inverted snob" said José.

"In what sense?" asked Sole, suddenly attentive.

"For example, a few months ago, a friend of mine was sitting next to Sax in church during a service and, running a finger lightly over the material of his jacket, which seemed threadbare, he asked him: 'Is this cashmere?' and Sax replied: 'Yes', as if annoyed by an obvious question. Do you see what I mean? Inverted snobbery is wearing a cashmere jacket as if it were any old rag."

From Provence I called a Scots friend, a literary agent who smokes a lot of cigarettes—Player's Plain—and drinks a lot of whisky. He is a friend of Sax. I told him of my useless attempts to meet and interview him, and the fact that—for one reason or another—I couldn't get the man out of my head. He suggested not to interview him, but to write a novel about him instead.

I could begin the story with his death: *Great artist found murdered in his studio*. The novel becomes an investigation. Readers always love crime stories. Years after, people are still wondering about Pasolini's death. "Who killed Sax?" I could look into the world of gambling or visit his many lovers, his illegitimate children, looking for some perverse, secret story … But was it possible that a controversial artist, censured, rich, famous, and even hateful in a certain sense, could be killed by someone who envied him? If the novel were a detective story, I would have to create the police inspector, describe the inquiry, his friends, enemies, family, the scandal, the inheritance … I will begin the story with Sax's murder in Holland Park. I have all I need: the victim, the crime scene and a line of investigation sufficient to make the plot a complex one. But what bothers me is the inspector. I don't want to invent an inspector because, however you describe him, he and the killer become the main characters, whereas all I'm interested in is Sax. I am interested in the artist, not his death. I am interested only in Sax because I realise I envy him, I envy the security of a talent confirmed by critics, collectors and market prices all over the world. The great, recognised artist is perhaps the only man who does what he wants, lives as he wants, while his life becomes a legend. Perhaps I haven't really admitted this even to myself, but I'd like my life to be a legend too. Besides, I have always felt indifferent towards people who are not extraordinary. My attention is not captured by success, but by someone's originality. I feel irresistibly attracted to those who are unique, solitary and always able to be themselves in any circumstances. It's not a question of heroes, but of people who choose to live their lives outside the canons of convention, without feeling that they are a part of the herd or protected by a social class or a political group. Certainly, if a person manages to make his mark and attain success while remaining entirely true to himself, then he has my admiration. And my envy too, unfortunately.

4

ROSSA

ROSSA IS A VERY BEAUTIFUL WOMAN. With her deep, green eyes, freckled skin and dark reddish hair, she looks Irish. Almost always cheerful and affectionate, she expresses herself with a sweet simplicity. She is intelligent and conceals an underlying vein of melancholy caused by the many sorrows of her life. This is why, even though she appears calm and smiling, she's a bit like a volcano, with unpredictable reactions. A setback or a misunderstanding can be enough to trigger an explosive outburst of rage that transforms her sweetness into an almost pitiless cruelty that she is unable to repress. I must admit that I really fear these sudden mood swings, because they spoil the harmony of our relationship and convey to me a sense of desperation, of profound disquiet, which then fades and is forgotten until the next explosion.

That day at Wilton's we were relaxed and talked of our affairs in great intimacy, as happens between husband and wife. The delightful thing about marriage is that there's no need to hurry. There is none of the stress of having to take leave of each other, of not knowing when you will see each other again. There is a tenderness, recreated every day, every night in bed and that is the basis of marriage. Sometimes you have to part, but this is followed by a return and you love each other even more. Disagreements lose their edge because neither of the two wishes to ruin a relationship made up of friends, habits common to both and a strength inherent to the couple. Husband and wife are united by many small things, such as, in our case, lunching at Wilton's and eating the same things every time, hoping that there will always be the same grilled sole, the same black bread, the puréed spinach, the chilled Chablis, a piece of Stilton to eat with celery and a glass of port. Marriage is not about novelty, and even the most curious people don't want novelty all the time. We grow fond of things that have been used, mended, resoled, repaired, because they have become truly ours.

That's why I like to be alone with Rossa. Looking at her, I realise that even though time has left its mark on her face, it is as if her beauty has grown, become more precious, more real.

We went to the Royal Academy, where there was a Matisse exhibition: pictures, drawings and fabrics. I knew that Rossa had a weakness for Matisse.

That evening Sole had organised a dinner, she wanted to introduce us to her friends. It was a sweet thought on her part. I like it when she includes us in her life. I know that growing up hadn't been easy for her, that my divorce from her mother had made her suffer very much. Rossa too felt that it had always been hard for her to win acceptance in life and gets furious when she feels that people don't appreciate her, or take her for granted. Rossa and Sole became friends, they understand and respect each other. They are both aware of their charm, but also insecure. And it is that insecurity that makes them so attractive.

Although I intend to shelve my obsession for Sax, I wonder why I am so drawn to painters and painting. Perhaps it's because they remind me of love stories. The most awful things can occur all around us, savage wars can break out, but a passionate affair lives beyond all laws because it has its own special laws. And the same holds for art. The First World War breaks out, there is the terrible battle of Verdun with its millions of dead and Matisse paints pictures that remind him of his winters in Tangiers, bowls of goldfish, piano lessons and portraits. During the Second World War, the photographer Brassaï used to go every day to Picasso's studio in rue des Grands-Augustins, while the city was under German occupation. In his diary he describes Picasso's chaotic habits, his secretary Sabartés, the cafés of Saint-Germain, Dora Maar—who had taken over from Marie-Thérèse Walter in his life—and a great exhibition of Matisse's work. You never sense the presence of the Nazis. The conversation is only about painting, models, friends and ideas, as if there were no war going on. Picasso had painted Guernica in that same studio.

Somewhat similarly, Sax lives and works indifferent to the world around him, except for his family and a handful of friends. He is immersed in his pictures and in his relations with his models, male and female alike. He works in extremely long sessions, with brief pauses. He portrays a humanity that is deformed, devastated, suffering, all fat and wrinkles.

I too would like to be a great artist and paint Rossa's portrait. I'd like to stay in the studio for hours looking at her, trying to discover her, interpret her. Perhaps I would arrive at a better understanding of that cheerful, elusive woman who loves to be alone and seems to prefer animals above all other things. A portrait with a black cat in her lap or nude with stray dogs. Every so often there would be breaks in which to make love and satisfy the intense desire that would have been aroused by my looking at her. I'm not very sure

I know what love is. In men, Rossa looks for the security she lost when her parents died. I don't know if she has abandoned all her men and if she is truly in love with me. I don't know why she decided to marry me of all people, as I am not a powerful or reassuring man. I am not a genius who could immortalise her forever. This is why I envy Sax. Through his work, he can dominate any woman: the most sophisticated, the most cultured, or the coarsest, who on seeing herself portrayed reacts with either love or hate, but in both cases feels mastered and flattered. Literature today no longer has that power.

"Would you have liked to be Amélie, Matisse's wife?" I asked Rossa.

"No, I'm happy to be your wife."

"Why?"

"I don't know, it was my choice and I'm fine like this. I want to be with you."

Rossa couldn't care less for all my fantasies about Sax, she doesn't give them a thought. Women are hard to decipher because they love strength, but weakness too. They want to be reassured, but also to reassure, they want to dominate but also to be dominated. A man can never really penetrate the mystery that is woman, understand all her fears, disappointments, hopes; he can never bridge the gap and does not have that mysterious and unpredictable *je ne sais quoi* that makes the heart beat faster and lends music to life. Perhaps the best way to live with a woman is to let yourself go, without trying to understand. No pleasure can be greater than the profound feeling of a love shared.

PART FOUR

TOWARDS ENVY

1

LONDON

I CAN'T GET SAX OUT OF MY MIND. If I ever write about him, I'd like my book to become as important as one of his paintings, I would like critics all over the world to discuss it. I would like it to arouse the curiosity of readers, who would say to themselves "It's a masterpiece!"

Taking advantage of the fact that Rossa wakes up late, the day after our arrival in London I went to Tony's early in the morning, without even knowing why, as if it were a ritual.

In the room where they serve breakfast I was caught on the wrong foot straight away. I saw Julian Sax talking to a rather chubby fortyish-looking woman with blondish hair, wearing a creased beige raincoat. She was writing things down in what looked like a school notebook, while he answered her questions. I sat down at the next table, which luckily was free, trying not to be noticed. Her accent said Oxford and an upper-class family background. In low, deliberately disagreeable tones, he was telling her why he had stopped gambling.

"There's no fun in it. Even if I lose it's all the same. No *frisson*."

"Are you very rich?"

"Very. But I already own two houses, a Bentley. All I do is work. I don't buy anything. Most of the time I don't even buy wine, people give it to me. When I was a playboy I gambled, I lost and I had no money. In fact I was in debt."

"Why did you have so many children?"

"I don't know. Maybe it's because I like making women pregnant."

"But that's irresponsible."

"Could be."

"Why do you make women suffer?"

" I don't know. It's not that I want to make them suffer. I am always sincere. I fall in love and at first I love them far too much, then I forget them."

"What, you forget them?"

"It's not my fault. It happens. At a certain point my attention wanders, love fades and I can no longer paint their portrait."

"Why? When you love a woman does she always become your model?"

"Usually, but recently I've been painting children, grandchildren, dogs and friends."

"And a very young female model too."

"Yes."

"Your paintings provide a detailed picture of a coarse, suffering, repugnant humanity. Fat, soft bodies, wearied by life, worn-out faces. Why?"

"Because that's how I see them, how I paint them. I don't need to deform them, make them abstract or grotesque as Picasso did."

"Wasn't Picasso a good artist?"

"I didn't say that."

"Who are the great artists?"

"Velázquez, Goya, Rembrandt."

"Have you read Bloom's book on Velázquez?"

"Yes, it says a lot about Bloom and little about Velázquez."

"Bloom has said that you are the Noel Coward of twentieth-century painting."

"Maybe because we were both photographed by Cecil Beaton. As a young man Bloom was slim, handsome, a playboy."

"And now?"

"He drinks, leads a boring life, and he's forever talking about his children."

"What relationship do you have with your children?"

"Weren't we supposed to be discussing my exhibition?"

"So, tell me, why did you choose to hold it in Venice?"

"Someone suggested the idea to my dealer, I'm not involved with such matters. A few months ago my assistant told me that a fellow had come looking for me. He wanted to suggest that I hold an exhibition in Italy. I didn't feel like talking to him. If I had to choose a place, I would go to Madrid, but I don't travel any more."

"Will you go to Venice for the opening?"

"No, that's quite out of the question. I must work, I have no time."

"Are you in love with your young female model?"

"No, I am painting her. Now, excuse me, but I have to finish her portrait. It has to be ready for the Venice exhibition."

As if seized by some fit he got up and went off without even saying goodbye.

With unexpected nonchalance, I went up to the journalist, who was sitting there flabbergasted.

"I'm sorry to disturb you, but was that Julian Sax you were talking to, by any chance?"

"Yes, it was," she replied, vexed not so much because I was bothering her but for the way in which he had left, indifferent, churlish.

"I was well aware that he is full of himself, a man who thinks he can use other people any way he feels! Luckily I took lots of notes."

"He is an extraordinary artist."

"He's not my type and what's more he was very cruel to a friend of mine. He is a perverse man, an egotist."

"But he is a great artist."

"They say that because he's the only survivor of his generation."

"Why did you interview him?"

"My editor asked me to. I didn't want to, but he persuaded me. I was prejudiced and I was right. I cannot bear ill-mannered, presumptuous people. But if you want to be a real professional then there cannot be any personal discriminations."

"My wife and daughter don't like him either."

"Do you know him?"

"No, but I know a lot about him."

"How is that?"

"Matteo Esse, an Italian art expert, and the Australian critic Charles Bloom have both talked to me a lot about him. But it's a long story."

"Do you know Bloom?"

"Yes, I met him two or three times in Madrid and New York. He is a very talented man with highly personal tastes."

"Sax just told me that he has become monot-onous."

"I don't know what he was like before, but he strikes me as a very intelligent man, with original ideas … not to mention an unexpected sentimental streak."

"Sax says he was a playboy."

"I wouldn't know. Matteo Esse wanted him to direct the Venice Biennale, but things didn't work out that way."

I was standing and the blonde journalist with her glasses, blue eyes and rather puffy face was looking at me without seeing me. Although her English was deliberately refined, it was as if she were talking to a taxi driver; she didn't ask me if I wanted to sit down, and I, so as not to interrupt the conversation, pretended I hadn't noticed her indifference and carried on talking to her as if we knew each other.

"Which paper is running your interview?"

"*The Sunday Times.*"

"Will you be going to Venice to see the exhibition?"

"I really don't think so and he's not going either. He's right, openings, especially your own, are frightfully boring. Moreover, if you are already the best paid artist in the world, what more could one wish for?"

"I confess that I am terribly envious of him, I'd like to write books as successful as his pictures. But I'll never succeed."

"I don't see what there is to envy in a person like that, who respects nothing and nobody. There is a limit even to egotism. Besides, in my view, he is not such a great artist and I'm not at all certain that he will go down in history. Of the English artists, together with Turner or Constable or Gainsborough, only Bacon will be remembered. He was far madder, intriguing and he had a superior talent. Oh, I'm sorry, my name is Tessa Evans."

"Giacomo Longhi."

"Are you Italian?"

"Yes."

"How lucky you are, I love Italy! I hate living here where it rains all the time. I'd like to go back to Rome or Kabul."

The talk moved on to Kabul, then Sarajevo, Rome. I was still standing, she was still sitting. At a certain point, as if she had suddenly awakened, she said in vexed tones:

"I must go, thanks, see you."

There is always something repressed about the way the English behave. In conversation they alternate moments of the most enjoyable good humour with sudden bursts of nervous irritability, almost intolerance. Tessa left Tony's, in a hurry, just as Sax had done shortly before.

I called Rossa on her mobile, but it was switched off, so I took a cab and asked to be taken to Jermyn Street, where I wanted to do some shopping. I chose two shirts, one blue and another with red and white stripes from Turnbull & Asser, and then a pair of black lace-up shoes, very simple, from New & Lingwood. I always buy the same things, as if I were afraid they might stop producing them.

London is a fantastic city for those little luxuries that still survive a great colonial empire. There is a lingering echo of a society that, although less wealthy than before, still cannot manage to forget its privileges.

Perhaps Sax had agreed to be interviewed by Tessa Evans because he was sensible of the fact that she belonged to the social class that had ruled the world a century before.

Basically, Sax was satisfied with his role as a great artist, capricious and irreverent towards anyone, including the royal family, whose portraits he had painted without making any compromises.

Tessa was a journalist from a good family who had chosen not to marry an English or Scottish aristocrat and to end up in a castle with lots of children, but to live independently, while conserving all the affectations of her social background. She didn't like Sax because, since he made portraits of the royal family, flirted with upper class girls, had millionaire friends and the tastes of a playboy, he wasn't the kind of man she could fall in love with. She was drawn to uncouth, coarse men who spoke English with a foreign accent and aroused in her the taste for an unconventional and, if possible, dangerous love affair.

Sax was born in Germany, but had become English, an English artist. He was not the real man, the hero, the revolutionary who would have made Tessa fall for him.

Rossa answered the phone, but I didn't tell her about the meeting with Tessa. All I asked her was if she wanted me to join her.

"Yes, at Emma Hope's. I'd like to buy some red shoes with really high heels."

2

SAX

S OLE SAID: "I saw Sax, a few days ago, at Damian's place. He was in the company of a young woman. We were sitting next to each other. He struck me as less unpleasant and we had a long talk."

"What does he talk about?"

"Gossip, children, friends."

"So you don't look down on him anymore?"

"I never looked down on him. He is an old man and I'm not sure if I like his work."

"What's the girl like?"

"Pretty."

"Do you think she is his girlfriend?"

"I don't know, I think she's his model."

3

THE SUNDAY TIMES

TESSA EVANS'S ARTICLE on Sax came out; it was fun, well written. She described the artist's work, his life, his family, his snobbery, his Anglophilia and wound up by justifying him because he is a German Jew who had to flee to England as a child with his parents, who had had to give up a glittering life in Berlin to become foreigners in London.

All the fault of Hitler and the race laws. As if that were not enough, Sax is the grandchild of a scientist who made some very important discoveries. Perhaps this is why he is so egocentric, vain and hooked on success, while looking down on everyone and everything at the same time. He has very little contact with his children and began painting their portraits only recently.

Tessa also told the story of the interview and the abrupt, rude way Sax had left. And then, she added: "Something surreal happened, as soon as Sax had left. I was approached by a stranger who asked me hundreds of questions about my interview with Sax. At the time, my thoughts were elsewhere, and I answered until, just as Sax had suddenly broken off his interview with me, I did the same with him. I have discovered that Sax is not only pursued by masochistic women of the English upper classes, but also by very inquisitive men." And so, Tessa admitted, the interview had been brilliant, given the interest it had aroused in a stranger. Besides, she asked herself at the end: "Who does one write for, if not for readers one doesn't know?"

To be considered a great writer, as Sax is considered a great artist, and presuming that I do in fact have a talent, I would have to follow his example: renounce my Italian culture, go to live in London or New York, become English or American, and get myself accepted in the English-speaking literary world.

But that world doesn't exist anymore, great writers and great publishers don't exist anymore, literary society doesn't exist anymore, and literature isn't fashionable anymore; the visual, plastic arts, the world of museums, art galleries, the great auctions, are at the centre of attention and attract large sums of money. This is why Sax is inaccessible. By now, although he has always gone against the flow, flying in the face of fashion, he has become a classic, one of the very few great living painters. Sax fascinates me because he is a part of an extinct race, that of the great personalities. Even in politics there are no more stars like Churchill. The last two legends were Mao and Kennedy. Fidel Castro is still alive, the last solitary survivor.

Frankly, I don't know why I feel so attracted to another man's life. I don't know why I prefer others to myself and find their destinies so extraordinary. I don't realise what I have. I look at life as if it were a show, a space of time in which what matters is not what you really think, but what you do, what you express, the places you go to, the things you leave behind. My life is like an obstacle course and I am always afraid of making a mistake, of losing, of being excluded. Sax has understood this perfectly, I think; that's why he works so obsessively on his pictures and drawings, and perhaps that's why he has had so many illegitimate children. He felt the need to disseminate himself excessively, the need to seduce women of all kinds and not to love any of them.

PART FIVE

THE GENESIS OF A NOVEL

1

LONDON

I HAVE COME TO THE CONCLUSION that if I am to begin my novel, Sax must leave reality and become a character. He is the linchpin around which the plot will be constructed. Where to begin? In his studio in London? At Tony's? The interview with the journalist from *The Sunday Times*? No, Rossa would be the journalist in my novel, she would ask him the questions while he tried to seduce her. Rossa would ignore his seductive ploys, he would lose patience and suggest that they go to his studio to see the painting he is finishing off. She would reply: "Maybe another time," accompanying her refusal with a catlike smile. Then he would get annoyed and take his leave. Afterwards he would call her, but she would not reply, obliging him to leave a message.

I don't know why, but as I thought of these things I was seized by nostalgia for some of the streets in Paris where I had lived many years ago. But above all I thought of a painter friend who has now disappeared from my life. I lived for a year in his house, in his studio. Come to think of it, while I have seen many of his paintings, and even owned one, I never saw him paint. He drank too much and when he was drunk he became melancholy. He was crazy for really young women, mad about them. He followed them all over the world, spent a lot of money and sold few pictures. He wished he was a great artist, but he didn't really believe it. He wasted too much time and there was no market for his work. I don't know what he thought of Sax; we used to talk of other things, women, books … Then, for no particular reason, we lost touch.

What do I want from Sax? Do I want him to become my friend, find me amusing, intelligent, interesting, special? Rather, do I want him to find my books special and then ask me to write one with him about his life, his art? To write a book with him would be a pretext to spend a lot of time together, to get to know each other really well. I would finally understand if he is a genius or a sham. I would like to devote some pages to his childhood in Germany and then the first years of his exile in England. I wonder if the Saxes had always spoken German in the family or if they spoke to their children in English with a German accent. But what do I care? It makes me think of how my grandmother spoke French. It is the fate of many Jews to speak with a foreign accent. Was Sax ashamed of coming from a German family? And what does this have to do with his painting, his art? It has a whole lot to do with it. His portraits of his aged, white-haired mother tell us many things about the artist and his feelings. In Sax's portraits of his mother a famous French art historian sees a tenderness, a humanity otherwise absent from his work.

So what will I write about Julian Sax? I don't know, I am deeply interested in him and every time I come across an article dealing with him I cut it out. I'd like to know everything about his life, but for no reason, almost like a reader of the glossies who follows the doings of the British royal family. It's a bit like that, but there's something else, especially a sense of guilt because I lack his courage. Giving up on life to be a great artist. He works while others talk about him. He must carry on painting, defying his age; he doesn't know how many more pictures he will be able to paint. What's more, old age makes him more fragile, he is unwell every so often and has to be admitted to hospital. He is arrogant but his dedication to work amends for that. But I, with the excuse that a writer must have many experiences, waste time on travel, inconsequential little jobs, and social engagements. I have never had the strength of character to be only a novelist, and to stop looking for other things. I have never been able to take chances, to go all the way, to measure myself against myself, my books. I am shy, I am afraid of suffering and I need to feel more secure about my talent, sell myself better.

Perhaps I'll never write Sax's biography, but if I did I would disagree with the idea that he is an English painter. He is a painter who uses English people, clothes, places and gardens, but at heart he has the feelings of a German Romantic. His is the spirit of *Immensee*, even though he won't hear of that and does his utmost to be remembered as a debauchee and a playboy. His model is Byron, but unlike his hero he cannot leave England because as a child he had to leave Germany. This is why he won't even live in Paris, because he's afraid of getting lost, of betraying his talent. He is an orderly, industrious man, something he needs on the one hand because it is his strength and on the other because it is the object of his scorn. That's why when he was still poor and less well known he gambled and drank like a madman. His work and his talent enabled him to love impossible or improbable women so he could prove to himself that he was no bourgeois, but transgressive, an artist and a rebel. An insolent man who doesn't believe in God and lives according to his moods. He wanted to become a great artist because he understood that this gave him the power he was looking for, the power to create and destroy his paintings, his friends and his women as he pleased. He knows he is not a likeable man, but he couldn't care less about that.

2

VENICE

I N VENICE THE TALK was all about the Sax exhibition. The Biennale was showing three paintings
and one triptych by Bacon. Who was the greater:
Bacon or Sax? A gallery owner said:

"One is a great artist, the other is a good painter."

I asked, "And Velázquez?"

"He was a great artist."

"So isn't Sax a great artist?"

"He's a good painter."

I went to see the Sax exhibition with Rossa and
a friend of ours. He criticised Sax's technique,
pointing out the flaws, the mistaken shadows; he
spared only a very few portraits, he was ruthless.
I was not very interested in his judgement. I knew
the history of many of the paintings and had

already seen them elsewhere. Rossa paid attention to his criticisms, but did not agree with them wholeheartedly. I let myself be carried away by the atmosphere of the entire work. In the first paintings you can still sense the influence of the German world, then you see that Sax had wanted to become English, a Londoner. The last picture on show was a portrait of a girl—Matteo Esse is sure to maintain that there are compositional errors, made up for by an extraordinary sense of youth. Esse is really enthusiastic about the exhibition, which he takes as an act of revenge that did justice to the world of contemporary art. Portraits of unknowns were mixed with those of other artists, of powerful men, animals and children. Sax was not in Venice but his dealer gave a dinner in his honour and the tables were enlivened by superb pink peonies, Rossa's favourite flower. But what was left for me to do? By now Sax had been consecrated in Italy too and the event that had prompted me to take an interest in him had come to pass. I knew that for a long time he had been misunderstood because his painting had been considered bourgeois, anti-revolutionary.

Figurative painters were beyond the pale, and this had always aroused the indignation of Matteo Esse and Charles Bloom. In those difficult years Sax continued to paint with perseverance. It took a long time before his family began to consider him a true artist. It was odd how Sax, on getting old, had grown like his works: he dressed in beige, white and ivory, the same colours as his portraits. For this reason the last self-portraits were ever more lifelike and you could see how the artist, who at seventy had painted himself nude, still vigorous, now preferred to appear dressed and almost diaphanous. His obsessive relationship with work was captured well by Bloom in an interview published in *La Stampa*, in which he said that Sax had not gone to Venice because he had no time to spare, because all his time, night and day, was devoted to work. Sax no longer went against the flow because he had won his battle. He had become like a great court painter of former times, like van Dyck, or Velázquez.

What I still don't know about him is his relationship with Judaism, of which virtually nothing is ever said. Maybe it's because he has flouted all the rules in this sense. Religious Jews are forbidden to reproduce human images, whereas he devotes himself chiefly to doing that. In Venice I talked with Sidney Wallace, his dealer, who asked me:

"Did you finally meet Sax?"

"Yes, with my daughter, last week, at Tony's. He told us he wasn't coming to Venice because he had no time to waste. He was in a good mood, he had just finished the portrait of the girl that is on show here at the exhibition."

I was lying, but I knew Wallace would not check up.

"He didn't come because he was unwell, he has been in hospital."

"When?"

"A month ago."

"But we saw him after that."

"Yes, perhaps he had just been discharged."

It was amusing to see how jealous Wallace was of his client. No one could know better than he what happened day by day in Sax's life. He attached enormous importance to being the best informed, the one who knew most.

3

NEW YORK

I WENT BACK TO NEW YORK on business and I chanced to bump into a very intelligent German publisher I have known for years because he was a friend of my father's. A man with an adventurous past, which he had always combined with the world of culture and business. He was said to be a great seducer.

Outwardly, he looks like a gentleman, or a fictional hero. He speaks English with a slight accent that makes his conversation even more attractive. He looks like a very wealthy man, although he isn't. But he has friends all over the world: politicians, bankers, great journalists, artists. His home is a beautiful house in Paris, and he is an enthusiastic opera lover. Fond of wearing flamboyant double-breasted pinstripe suits, he is considered an amusing man, a true cosmopolitan and is invited for weekends to the most exclusive country houses.

We had a drink in the hotel bar. He talked to me about literature and music. I told him that I had seen Julian Sax's exhibition in Venice and that maybe I was going to start writing a novel about him.

"But why? It's not worth the effort! He's not very interesting. He doesn't warrant a novel. There are plenty of other subjects. Write a thriller, write a book about the people you have met, on your relationship with Judaism! At most you can write a short story about Sax, but believe me, not even that is worth the effort."

"But he is a great artist!"

"So they say, but he is a person of little interest, very little indeed."

I realised that it was time to change the subject and that he wasn't going to be the publisher of my book.

I must say that the German publisher's remarks about Sax puzzled me. Probably his judgement was subjective, motivated by old affairs with women or by jealousy over such an explosive and unexpected success. Many say that Sax pretends to be an ascetic, that he only thinks of painting, whereas in reality he is a worldly, superficial man. But what does that matter? I continue to meet people who talk about him to me, but I can't get my novel started because I don't have a plot. I thought of having Rossa take a fancy for Sax, which would lead to my jealousy. She could become his model and something might grow up between them, but it's a banal storyline; by now he has had many models, too many.

Do I envy his freedom in love? His success? His money? No, I envy his strength of character, his perseverance, his arrogance, his talent. His constant desire to paint another portrait. I find it extraordinary that his paintings are snapped up at astronomical prices by great collectors and by the world's most important museums. Sax devotes all his time to painting, trying to interpret a face, a body, a place. His work reveals a great tenderness for animals and a meticulous, almost excessive attention for his human models. No destiny seems to me more enviable than that of an artist who can permit himself to observe the world around him and to reproduce it in his own way.

4

ROSSA

A T THE END OF JULY I TOOK ROSSA to Paris, where we had not been for a long time. We stayed in a little hotel in Saint-Germain-des-Prés. I wanted to feel free in a place where writers are respected, where many important books have been written. The list of artists who lived and worked in Paris during the twentieth century is endless and even though that world has now disappeared completely, you still breathe in an atmosphere that, every so often, I feel a need for. It's still possible to sit down in a café, order a drink and write for hours without being disturbed. The truth is that I went there because, as I obsessed over the possibility or not of writing a book about Sax, I had the feeling I had lost my way. I was confused. So I decided first of all to recover possession of my identity as a writer.

As soon as we arrived we went out for a stroll. I told Rossa that I consider rue Visconti the most beautiful street in the world. She seemed puzzled. I pointed out a small two-story house where Racine died in 1675. Then I took her to rue des Grands-Augustins, where Picasso used to live.

The next day, we had lunch at Benoît's, an old restaurant, with two French friends. We were talking about literature and one of them, a refined intellectual who teaches in the United States, came out with a violent tirade against Sartre:

"If French literature has gone stale, it's partly his fault. He left a blot of black ink. His pupils are intelligent, but who gives a damn for intelligence? You have to be much more than that. Kundera is a novelist, but he's not French. There aren't any writers like Gide any more!"

Rossa had fun, but she is worried by other things, she is afraid of fanatical Islamic fundamentalism that, according to her, could trigger a total war.

On our way back to the hotel, in rue de Seine she asked me:

"Where can you live in peace?"

"In Patagonia," I replied without hesitation.

And she:

"My sister always wanted to send our brother Massimo to Patagonia!"

A bomb could destroy the museums, the paintings, the monuments. I knew this well because years before I had been in Afghanistan and I had seen the destruction of the Buddhas of Bamiyan.

Walking along the Quai Voltaire, I showed Rossa Sennelier, an old shop that sells canvases, colours, pencils, brushes and turpentine. It was very hot and Rossa was walking idly, a little indolent. I found her more and more beautiful. We had been making love for many years and ours was like a long amorous conversation, without interruptions.

She has really beautiful long legs, and a wonderful little mouth. She still smelled like a child and had an attractive, good smile. She was a woman who loved to laugh and have fun and she never talked of her sorrows. If need be, she would keep her distance, and she was never indiscreet. Without a doubt she was vain and liked to look at herself naked in the mirror, to see that her body was still young, enviable. A solitary person, she detested social life. But she loved to dance; it was as if she had a drop of African or Brazilian blood, which sometimes made her uncontrollable, wild. We would talk a lot but we could be silent too. In the early days of our relationship we used to argue, but then the fights grew fewer and we learnt to understand each other. We didn't want anyone to interfere with our life.

We felt so good in Paris that I would have liked to stop time, so that summer would never end. The thought of the short, cold winter days made me feel terribly sad.

During those days I would have liked to be able to paint Rossa's portrait, but the truth was that I had another vice, that of giving my pen free rein and inventing stories. To capture on paper a state of mind, a place, a thought. Perhaps I could have portrayed Rossa better with a pen than with brushes. She could become my model for a book.

It would have been much better to drop Sax and get inside the head of the woman I loved. She was elusive when I asked her about past affairs. All I got was sketchy allusions. Sometimes, if she told me of certain things in her life before we met, I would be amused; at other times I grew jealous because I couldn't bear the idea that she had had other men, other experiences before me. Life as a couple is like that. What counts is your partner's story, because you already know the truth about yourself. We all recount our past in our own way. I remember that Rossa attached great importance to her photographs, which she guarded jealously. One day, as we were watching a scene from a film by Truffaut, in which the leading lady was cutting up some photographs with scissors, she had said to me:

"You shouldn't cut them up, it's like erasing fragments of your own life. You destroy them and all the evidence is gone for ever."

PART SIX

LISA AND TED

1

PARIS

ONE AFTERNOON, when we were out for a walk, Cesare called. He is a handsome man, tall, blond, intelligent and ambiguous. He never wants to bring anything to a conclusion. When an idea takes concrete form, he becomes elusive. One of his favourite expressions is:

"I've got a whole lot of new things to tell you, interesting stuff. Whenever the time is right, we can talk things over at our leisure."

Cesare sometimes declares that he wants a certain job and as soon as someone makes the effort to get it for him, he says that he's not interested in the slightest and, to the contrary, he would rather do without it. His worldview and his life do not involve plans. Cesare is also an extraordinary collector of objects and friends. Of himself he always says: "I who am not". For Cesare things should never have a purpose. Death is a subject that doesn't scare him, it's as if it didn't concern him. His chosen role is always to be argumentative and disagreeable and he takes an excessive interest in the most unpredictable things, but then he gets bored and his attention wanders. For example, as soon as he buys an apartment somewhere, that place immediately bores him. In short, he is a spoilt man, but certainly one with no lack of charm and intelligence.

Cesare is a great friend of Rossa's, and he has always admired her. Perhaps he is in love with her; he trusts her, and wishes her well. In her he sees a blend of two qualities he considers essential— beauty and intelligence. He, who is usually so intolerant of women, who strike him as obstacles between him and freedom, smiles when he talks about Rossa. And it was he who told me one day:

"Giacomo, have you ever had an affair with Rossa? You should, she's a really beautiful woman."

I shall always be grateful to him for that wise and generous advice.

He asked me:

"Where are you?"

"In Paris."

"Why don't you come to Capri? I'm staying at Dino's, it's simply wonderful!"

I thought that on Capri I might put my thoughts in order and start to write.

2

CAPRI

WE ARRIVED ON THE HYDROFOIL from Mergellina. The weather was overcast, just a glimpse of a pale sun without enough strength to penetrate the greyish-purple mass of clouds that blended with the colour of the sea. Cesare came to pick us up at the Marina Grande. He had the cheerful air of someone who has been on holiday for days, slept lots, and feels wonderful. The house was pleasant, surrounded by white, purple and pink bougainvillea and other flowers with a very summery scent. Everything was ripe and warm. From the terrace of the house you could see the Faraglioni rocks and hear the sound of the sea, the engines of the boats and the chirruping of the crickets. We instantly fell in with the rhythms of the long, slow days, punctuated by meals and sleep. Rossa was happy, she read the papers with her usual meticulous attention, following the Bank of Italy affair, the scandals and the phone tapping. Cesare was idly reading a book and criticising events in Rome. There were many American tourists on the island and you heard English spoken everywhere. Rossa and I went for long swims and tried not to eat too much, but we couldn't resist the pizza and the local Falanghina wine. The nights on Capri were warm, star-filled, indulgent.

I knew right from the first day that I was about to begin my novel. A character like Cesare was beginning to take shape, but he was a killer: he passed himself off as an art dealer, frequented high society, but he always carried a concealed pistol, a Luger, with which he killed his victims. His was a vice. He wanted revenge, to demonstrate his hatred of humanity, which had disappointed him. He was a killer who killed for pleasure, not for necessity. He despised the murderers who hit the headlines, couldn't stand the underworld and detested any kind of affiliation, be it political, religious, or ideological. He was a dandy who, rather than play the violin or write poetry, killed people. Irresistibly attracted to risk, he managed to elude all investigation, ensuring that he was never suspected or arrested. Basically, he enjoyed killing the way a gambler enjoys gambling. He didn't want to get caught, and would have preferred to die in a shoot out. Nor did he want to end up in the promiscuity of a prison, mixing with the other convicts and listening to their life stories. He was an immoral man who lived for the day and took death for granted.

This was what I was thinking of writing there on Capri. In the meantime I idly savoured our holiday. For hours I would sit watching and listening to the sea, the gulls. All around me I could smell lemons, tomatoes, rocket, basil and rosemary. Capri is a place where you learn to live among a superabundance of smells: flowers, sugar, fish. It's an island where you walk a lot and a place that induces thought, a place where local people remember you and greet you warmly.

The character I was daydreaming about fascinated me, but first of all I needed to master a language of which I knew nothing. I would have to learn how to set up a murder, how to shoot, how to leave no traces and how to avoid wiretaps.

An assiduous newspaper reader like Rossa, who preferred the crime pages, would have been useful to me. I would use her as a consultant as well as a character. Her name would be Lisa and she would become Cesare's ideal woman. Cesare's name would be Ted. I had found two perfect names and created two characters suitable for a murder story, but it had to be clear that Ted's heroes were not criminals, but libertines. The intervals between one murder and the next could be very long. Ted resembled Cesare physically and like him he was an elegant, inquisitive man, who spoke languages well. But being an unpunished murderer requires qualities of perseverance and concentration that Cesare didn't possess. Although Ted killed only seldom, by now he had committed many crimes and Interpol was on his trail. It was known that there was an 'uncatchable' killer, who seemed to kill at random, without a motive. He chose his victims on a whim, as Sax did with his models.

That was when Sax came back to my mind and everything began to come together and take shape. He too would become a character in the story I was on the point of writing.

The book would begin in London, at a party where Ted meets an Englishwoman who talks to him about a lady friend of hers who had given up everything for love of a great artist, Julian Sax. She had lived with him in a house where he had painted her, tormenting her, for two years, only to leave her without any explanation. He had registered the house where they had lived together in her name, but he had gone. He never returned, nor did he answer her calls. He didn't want to see her again. Ted, who knew who Julian Sax was, would feel an immediate curiosity about that woman.

On listening to her friend's story, a cold shiver would run down his back and he would feel an instinctive dislike for Sax. The tale of a woman abandoned by her lover mattered nothing to him, but he hated the arrogance of those who think they can do what they wish while riding roughshod over other people's feelings.

Ted would meet Lisa and realise that she was shy, still in love and suffering over what had happened. So he would ask her many things about Sax, his behaviour and what kind of man and lover he was. How many pictures, how many drawings had he made using her as a model? Had he given her any portraits? He would want to know what they talked about, what had Lisa's relationship with Sax's children been like. Why had they not had a child together?

Ted and Lisa would meet on other occasions, dinner at the Poissonerie or the Caprice. Lisa would get interested in this new friend who took life as a light, amusing thing. Sax had been a devil, Ted was an angel who had fallen into her life and he had a rare quality in a man—he could listen to a woman without interrupting her, showing real interest in what she was saying.

Ted would be enchanted by Lisa. She was very beautiful and although she only spoke to him of another man and of her romantic misadventure

with him, she did so with moral elegance and ex-
pressed herself with charm. It was sad that such a
young, delicate woman had allowed herself to be
deceived by such a perverse man, well aware of how
their affair would end. Sax was known for his habit of
taking women to pieces. Lisa could not resign herself
to the idea of no longer sharing his life and his days:
she knew he was wicked and dangerous, but he had
painted her, immortalised her forever. No one else
would ever do that. When he was still in love with her
and they worked and slept together, she was dazzled
by his talent and didn't want to notice time passing.
She felt she was the only woman who would stay
with him always. Ted wanted to know every detail
of the affair between Julian and Lisa and he realised
how the artist had stolen her heart. Competing with
a genius wasn't going to be easy, also because his real
'talent' had to remain in the shadows.

He would ask Lisa where Julian lived and she
would tell him that she knew everything because a
girlfriend spied on him for her. He lived in a certain
street and every day, at the same time, he would eat
at Tony's. She knew that, after leaving her, he had

had a passionate affair with a coloured woman. He had painted her and ditched her and now he was living with a very young girl.

Ted would go to Tony's where he would see Julian with a brunette, pregnant, who was perhaps one of his daughters. He would observe him and find him an interesting man, dressed with the calculated but sophisticated negligence of the artist. He would notice his penetrating, ironic gaze, his impatient hands toying with his tortoise shell glasses or picking idly at his food, listening to the young woman's talk, sometimes laughing, sometimes absent.

Ted would not try to approach him, but would tail him obsessively, memorising what he did, the hours he kept and his habits.

He would begin to understand why Lisa talked of Julian with so much enthusiasm, why she stubbornly continued to think about this diabolical old man, so tenacious and despotic in his work, with his manias and his rules for living, thus reducing him, Ted, to a mere go-between. As long as Julian was around, Ted would not exist for Lisa as far as love was concerned. This thought was a torment for him because he felt he was the right man, the one who could make her forget Sax. He would have to be very patient and persevering. Insinuate himself into Lisa's life, day after day, until he became indispensable.

But Sax had to die, to disappear. Only after his death would Ted win Lisa.

He would kill him without remorse. The time had come to punish Sax once and for all, to punish a man who thought he was invulnerable and omnipotent only because he had a great talent. His pride knew no bounds and his ascetism concealed something frivolous and overstated. He used people weaker than himself to feed his own legend. Lisa was one of the many victims who had let themselves be dominated in the belief that he was a genius, but Ted knew that this wasn't so. Sax lacked that ingenuousness, that passion, which only true geniuses possess. There was too much effort, too much will, too much fussiness in the way he worked. Moreover, he had become a fixture in the society columns and gloried excessively in his reputation as a perverse womaniser.

Early one August morning, Ted would leave Julian Sax dead on the pavement with one unerring shot. As soon as he committed the crime, Ted would race nimbly across the park and down into the tube before catching a train, followed by the ferry. He would throw his Luger into the Channel. As soon as he got to France, Ted would go back to London and the next day he would talk to Lisa about the murder, trying to console her and to understand with her who had killed Sax.

By now I had the plot in mind, as well as the characters. The story of a murderer who kills to defend the honour of a woman whose feelings had been trampled on by an artist. All I had to do was get to work and write it. The novel called for a slow rhythm. Even though the plot was simple, the characters were complex and so the tale had to be told in its own time if it was to unfold in a credible way. The reader, on discovering that Ted was a murderer, would have to swing between the desire that he redeem himself and manage to win Lisa,

119

and the taste of witnessing the birth of a decision to commit a crime. The appeal of the story lay in the fact that it was both romantic and passionate, dark and full of shadows. My subconscious would emerge and it would be clear why I was obsessed with Sax, why I envied a man who lived a monastic life in London painting portraits that an American art dealer sold for millions of dollars. My envy and admiration for him had prompted me to create Ted, who would become my alter ego, my personal avenger. I would transform Rossa into Lisa because only in a novel could I accept her becoming a model for Sax, but I would revenge myself by having him killed. For her part Lisa should not seem a naive victim, quite the contrary; she was a very special, stubborn woman who didn't want to resign herself to being abandoned and who, unconsciously, inspired her admirer to avenge her. The description of the crime would have to be accurate, plausible. That was why I had to go to check out every detail: Sax's house, Tony's, the pavement, the building opposite, the shops next door, the restaurants where Ted would take Lisa to try to seduce her.

3

LONDON

REMEMBERING THAT CESARE owned a small apartment in St James's, I asked him if Rossa and I could stay there. He gave us the keys gladly, unaware of my plans.

The apartment could easily have been Ted's. Wallpaper with stripes in a shade of burgundy, antique furniture, pictures by minor artists of the Italian *seicento*, Afghan carpets. There was a small, dark ante-room, a living room with two leather armchairs, a desk, two bedrooms, a bathroom and kitchen. It was the perfect place for Ted, who had to have the same tastes and manias as Cesare. There, he would prepare to murder Sax.

I took Rossa to lunch at Tony's and we saw Sax. He was alone, relaxed, leafing through a newspaper. He didn't notice our presence, and I tried to memorise every detail of the place and to capture every expression on his face. I thought that the man sitting in front of me, who with a simple and natural gesture was dunking a biscuit in his tea, was a great painter, old by now, whose paintings are recognised everywhere. People would say:

"That's a Warhol, a Van Gogh, a Goya, a Caravaggio, an Antonello da Messina, a Sax".

There he was, fragile, defenceless, and observing him aroused a different emotion in me compared to the other times. Who was I to decide to kill him, even through a novel and a fictional character like Ted? I began to realise that Ted would not do it because, as he was preparing to commit the crime, to eliminate his rival for ever and avenge Lisa's offended love, something would make him see that he couldn't do it. Killing Sax would not be right, it wouldn't bring him luck. Besides, wasn't it absurd to think of winning a woman by killing the man she was in love with? Death would make him a hero, an irreplaceable memory, while all he would be for Lisa was a friend unable to console her.

No, Ted would understand that Sax ought to be challenged. He would have to let him know, through mutual acquaintances, that a young man, very rich and seductive, was winning Lisa, who had got over things, was blooming again and having the time of her life. This would certainly upset Sax. A slap in the face to his vanity. But was Sax a jealous man? And was Ted capable of falling in love with someone? Was it possible for him to imagine living with a woman? Would he be able to give up being a criminal, working only as an art dealer and living a normal life? Was he sure he could control the urge to kill? Ted would understand that in reality Julian had loved Lisa and his pictures bore witness to that love. But, at a certain point, he could no longer live with her, he needed new emotions, and his attention had shifted to a fat black woman who aroused an incontrollable sexual desire in him and this too was borne out by the portrait he had made of her.

Lisa should not be consoled, but seduced. In his way, Ted too was an artist. He had to tell her that he was a killer wanted all over the world. This might terrify her, but perhaps her curiosity would be aroused and she would fall in love with him. But he wouldn't trust Lisa completely, just as he didn't trust anyone. He had gone unpunished because he had chosen a solitary life and he would never let his secret out. He couldn't do that, he could not fall in love, nor could he kill an artist. A great criminal must know his own limitations. But if Ted didn't kill Sax and if he gave up the idea of winning Lisa's love, how would the book end? With no crime and no *coup de théâtre* would the novel still hang together? On the contrary, the strength of the story would be that of setting itself up as the great novel of seduction, envy and passion that I had in mind. The storyline would be charged with tensions right to the finish. Only when the perfect crime was ready to be committed would Ted change his mind. Lisa would never be his.

It was certainly a very particular situation. We were at Tony's, Rossa was eating a salad while I bit into a hamburger. In front of us was Julian Sax, taking the last sips of his tea and leafing through the newspaper. He could never have imagined what had been going through my mind over all those months. He didn't know that I envied him, that he had become my obsession, that he had inspired me to write a book and that only a moment before I had decided that Ted would not kill him. He didn't know that Lisa would always love him. Luckily, Rossa too was unaware of all this. She would have to wait until she read the novel.